'Soul Tax:
A Novella'
Copyright © Tadhg Culley 2021.
Cover Image: Cottonbro at Pexels

Contact the author at:
undotheheartbreak@gmail.com

ISBN: 9798471320093

part one

Dust erupts in a network of tunnels as a group of American paranormal investigators creep through the cavernous cellars of what was once an English Victorian Institute. It is now a museum of sorts and they have been given permission to do their all-night supernatural investigation. They are into the very early morning hours as Shay, the fifty-year-old star and owner of international YouTube sensation 'Shay's Spirit Tourists' leads the ghost hunt. He is rumoured by the spiritual community to be something of a charlatan, in it only for the internet fame, views and advertising revenue he earns from his channel. He leads the search with a flashlight as his wife, Deborah, in her late forties and a bossy, attention seeker, holds onto Shay's jacket from behind, evidently unnerved by this site. Bryan follows her, a forty-year-old, respectful and well-respected Medium, and unnervingly even he appears on edge. Most of their fanbase tunes in for him, since he gives the group some credibility, as the sensationalist antics of the married couple often get on the nerves of the viewers but always ensure fresh eyes from clickbait.

Behind them, Leti, a twenty-two-year-old inexperienced and vulnerable newbie to the scene, clutches the hand of her boyfriend, Aaron, who is two years older than her, along only for the ride since he is a fearless skeptic.

That forms the core team of 'Shay's Spirit Tourists', though they often invite local guests wherever they visit on their ghost tours. This international event has been attended by thirty-year-old Rob, the only Englishman present, who is a apparently a bit of a freeloader keen to serve his own ambitions. He kicks up dust with his boot, films with a night vision camera and jokes around, "Look... Orbs..."

Leti coughs, pulls an inhaler from her bag and uses it. Aaron puts his arm around Leti and barges Rob ahead. Bryan warns the group, "Enough. I sense a growing malice in the vicinity".
Shay guides the group into a cellar chamber with fearless, childish excitement, "Perfect. Get in. Quietly".
Deborah, Bryan, Leti, Aaron and Rob funnel into the tiny area...

Aaron complains, "It's a bit of a tight fit".

Rob jokes, "That's what she said!".

Deborah grabs Rob's arm as he holds the camera, "Stop pissing about. Get footage for the channel. The less talking from you, the better".

They kneel and sit in the sandy cellar chamber.

Shay begins his séance, "Spirit, we are humbled by your presence. I wish to push further as I feel your strength growing..."

Shay picks up a pebble from the ground, "I'll throw this pebble outside the chamber. I want you to throw it back. Got me in focus, Rob?".

Rob jests, "Yeah, you look like Brad Pitt... If he put on sixty pounds".

Shay raises his eyebrow, "...Spirit, I'm throwing the pebble now".

Shay throws the pebble out of the chamber into the tunnel. They hear the pebble hit a wall. The group grows anxious.

Something throws the pebble back into the room! It rolls through the sand in front of Shay. Leti squeals. Shay laughs.

Leti whispers, "Oh my God. Oh my God, it's happening..."

Shay asks, "Did you get that in frame?".

Rob answers, "Fuck me. Er... Yeah... Got it... This is goin' viral".

The group moves further into the chamber, away from the door, unsurprisingly unnerved by whatever has followed them down to the tunnels... Or whatever was present before they got down here...

Bryan warns, "Shay—"

Shay ignores, "Thank you, Spirit. Let's get even more activity" and reaches for the pebble to throw it again, sensing how many more subscribers tonight's episode will be netted by this sensationalism.

Bryan advises, "Let's call it a night".

Shay barks, "Hell no. This is EXACTLY why we're here".

Leti complains, "It's freakin' me out, guys".

Rob searches outside with the night vision viewfinder: Nothing is seen but dust in the air of the tunnel.

Shay implores, "Emerge, Spirit. We feel your force. Come!".

Shay throws the pebble out of the room again. The pebble flies back inside and hits Shay's jacket harder.
Deborah gasps, "Amazing".
Leti begs, "Please stop".
Shay boasts, "Oh, we ain't seen nothing yet—"

Scratches at a large stone block on the floor are heard.

Shay scoffs at the Spirit to try and get better reactions for his vlog, "Spirit... This is pathetic. You're weak. Pebble barely touched me. Show us your true strength. Or are we stronger than you because we are still alive?"

...Silence.

Leti panics, "Spirit's gone. Let's get ou—"

The block flies through the air and caves in Shay's skull! The crew members flee for their lives and escape the room as fast as they can. Rob drops the camera.

It films as blood leaks from Shay's head into the sand.

ONE WEEK EARLIER:

Red wine pours into a plastic cup that rests on a fold-down table of an aircraft during mid-flight. An Air Hostess smiles as she serves Shay the drink. Shay lifts the cup to toast the group. Deborah, Bryan, Aaron and Leti raises their cups together.

Shay toasts, "To greater heights! See what I did there?".
The group clinks their cups together and guzzles alcohol.
Deborah celebrates, "The international circuit awaits. We're about to go big. Break into the global circuit... We deserve it, guys. Remember that... You've been with us since Day One. Enjoy the show!".
Shay slurs, "With much still to be discovered..."

Deborah gets back to her magazine: 'Psychic Tomorrow'. Shay gets the Air Hostess to pour him another cup of wine, intending to get very drunk on this flight. He may deal with the spirits of another realm as his day job and bread and butter, but he absolutely hates heights with a fierce passion. He was not embarrassed when he asked if there was any other way to get to England from America other than by flying. Put off by the fact it would take so much longer by boat, he was forced to face his fears. Now he intends to see the bottom of a bottle or two... (Or even three).

Bryan puts on an eye mask, adjusts his chair back and sleeps. Leti pulls out a scrapbook from her seat pouch. She flicks it open to a handwritten family tree of the 'Lloyd' surname. Aaron leans over to view the pages.
Aaron whispers, "Didn't know you had family in England, babe".
Leti answers, "Not living. Just ancestors".
Deborah boasts, "We'll help you communicate, dear".
Shay suggests, "Might as well kill two birds with one stone".
Shay guzzles more wine and reaches over to close the window blind so he no longer has to see the sheer drop through the clouds. Doing so, he manages to spill red wine down his shirt. It looks like blood...

After a long flight with its fair share of turbulence and a sketchy landing that had Shay praying to the Heavens, 'Shay's Spirit Tourists', leave the British airport and carry backpacks and suitcases behind them. Rain drenches all of their belongings, along with them. A tour bus awaits in a bay and Rob opens the doors, gesturing to the airbrush painting on the side of the bus: It depicts Shay with a magic ball as lightning and mist surrounds him with text: 'Shay's Spirit Tourists. GUARANTEED Paranormal Experiences. BOOK NOW: 00666 333 666.' Rob sparks up a cigarette and outstretches a hand to Shay.
Rob sarcastically greets him, "Welcome to England. The land of fine weather and gorgeous food..."
Shay complains about the bus painting, "Could've got my nose right".
Rob shakes hands with Shay and Deborah, "Good to finally meet you both. Big fan of your channel. Heard so much about you too..."

Deborah frowns, "Hmm. You look nothing like your profile pic".

Rob points at the bus painting, "I'm not blessed with your husband's good looks. Anyway, being a psychic and all, you can't be surprised by my looks, right? I would've thought you could've seen me with your third eye..."

Deborah claims, "Trust me, dear, it doesn't work like that. I wouldn't lower myself to trick out my trade as if it was a mere gimmick".

Shay introduces Rob to the others, "Meet Rob. Our driver".

Rob implies, "Hoping to be more than that. I can be your tour guide too. Know the area well. I have some ideas of my own. Hi everyone".

Rob shakes hands with Bryan, Aaron and Leti.

Shay thrusts his suitcase at Rob. The group boards the bus. Rob's cigarette gets soaked. He throws it away and begrudgingly loads the bus with the group's belongings, "Cheeky bloody yanks".

Rubbish litters the tour bus. Clearly it is a second-hand rush job. The group takes their seats and gets as comfy as they can. Aaron picks up an empty snack packet.

He jokes, "Living the high life, eh?"

Shay teases, "Wait and see where we're headed".

Rob boards the bus, shakes off the rain and grins.

The tour bus leaves the airport as a plane takes off. They ride along motorways as the Americans soak up the sights of English countryside. Sheep and cows, rolling hills, odd cottages and more pubs than the eye can see. That evening, still on the tour bus after yet another long journey, Shay stands in the aisle and claps his hands. Bryan wakes from his slumber and wipes dribble from his chin. Deborah giggles as she films Bryan. She turns the camera to Aaron and Leti as they wake up in each other's arms.

Shay gives a speech, "Time to show you what this country's all about. No working on our first night. Relax, it's on me. But remember. Our audience wants the real deal. We've done all we can in America. This calling we have to foreign shores brings us to a far more ancient land. Never drop your guard, even on a night off. We don't really know what we're up against just yet. Spirit always seeks out those sensitive to it".

Deborah cheers, "Let the feather pillows wear off the jet lag!".
The group wolf-whistles and applauds.
Aaron whispers to Leti, "If it's like this tour bus, get ready to fight off
bed bugs…"

The tour bus rolls onto the grounds of a brooding, Gothic mansion
hotel built in the 17th Century. A river weaves its way through the rustic
estate. A chapel nestles amongst shrubbery. The tour bus parks in
front of the mansion. Rob hops out, opens the side door and unpacks
luggage. Bryan and Deborah disembark and head for the hotel
reception.
Deborah gasps at the impressive surroundings, "Oh, wow".
Bryan claims, "It's like, 'The Haunting'. Remember Hill House? I
watched that film way too young when I was a kid. People think that's
why I ended up as a Medium! As if I was scarred for life!".
Aaron and Leti exit the bus. Aaron jokes, "Hugh Crain's gonna get ya!
Now you're in England. He's waited all this time for this moment…"
Leti shudders at the thought. Aaron grabs their bags.
Aaron whispers to her, "No way is this just a treat. Shay's as tight as a
fish's ass. And that's watertight! Remember how he is whenever we
try to claim expenses? Ain't no way this is 'on him' without a clause".
Leti points at the airbrush painting, "Your Uncle's quite the silver fox.
Must run in the family".
Aaron jokes, "More like a silver goat".
Shay hops off the bus. He coincidentally chews candy like a goat and
admires the massive airbrush painting of himself.

In the Gothic Mansion Reception, a Hotel Receptionist, impressively
dressed in formal attire, hands Deborah several room keys. Leti gasps
in awe at the grandeur of the antique decorations. She thinks, *It truly is
fit for royalty. Nothing like this exists in America. This is straight out one of
those gothic paperbacks you used to read as a teen. The ones with a
terrified woman, barely clad, on the front, running away from a sinister
looking mansion… Just look at it. It's like stepping into history. This is the
closest to Time Travel you are ever gonna get, girl.*
The group makes their way up the archaic staircase…

Leti and Aaron reach the top and amble along a corridor with oak panel walls as wooden floorboards creak beneath a red carpet. Shay jingles a set of keys outside a bedroom doorway.

Shay jests, "Here boy. Come and get it".

Aaron wrestles with luggage and frowns at Shay. Shay throws the keys at Aaron and they hit him in the cheek.

Shay laughs, "Fetch! Good boy… By the way, you two lovebirds have the Honeymoon suite. You can thank me later. "Nudge Nudge Wink Wink"…"

Shay marches down the corridor and around a corner. Aaron juggles the luggage and grabs the keys from the floor.

He sighs, "You'd think I was the Uncle".

Leti admires the carved sign outside their room that reads 'Kingmaker's Chamber'.

Leti gasps, "There's no way you're still grumbling? Just look around you! Give him some credit. This place is amazing. It's like we're in a Victorian novella… Just close your eyes and imagine…"

Aaron moans, "No thanks. Victorians give me the creeps. That was the Jack the Ripper era that ruined my childhood… My Grandma loves all those serial killer books and they were always strewn about the house when I was a wee nipper. I stumbled across one of those things aged five… And let me just say, the first thing a kid looks for in a book is photos… And unfortunately for me, there were plenty of black-and-white photos of murder victims and crime scenes and… Oh man.. You never forget that… Especially aged five… THANKS GRANDMA!".

Aaron fights off a shiver up his spine, almost drops the luggage again and approaches Leti with the keys in his teeth.

He mumbles, "Anyway, you don't know him like I do. There's always a catch when it comes to Uncle Shay…"

Leti giggles, "Never look a gift horse in the mouth", as she pulls the keys from Aaron's mouth and unlocks the door. He bites at her as if he was an angry horse…

Leti casts open the chamber door to reveal the grand and majestic Medieval themed architecture of the honeymoon suite. A four-poster bed fit for a King and Queen stands at one end with steps that lead up to it. Red velvet drapes hang from the ceiling as medieval weaponry decorates the walls. A full suit of armour stands guard.

Leti gasps in amazement, "Wow, just look at that".

Aaron winks, "Check out that bed".

Leti chuckles, "Dream on if you think you're sleeping in it with me".

Leti kisses a crucifix that hangs on a necklace and giggles.

Elsewhere, Shay and Deborah get comfy in their modest double room. Meanwhile, Bryan and Rob set up camp in their twin room. Rob places his laptop on the desk, "No rest for the wicked".

Bryan states, "Shay said work's off limits".

Rob retorts, "No harm gettin' a head start. First impressions and all".

Inside the Kingmaker's Chamber, Leti stretches on the four poster bed like a cat. Aaron sets up a camper bed at the opposite end of the room, gutted that he can't unwind on the focal point of the room. Leti gazes out of a window at the expansive grounds below.

Leti begs, "Let's go and explore".

Aaron puts on an English Butler accent, "Right away, your Highness".

Darkness descends across the Gothic mansion estate. Aaron and Leti meander across the grass lawn that runs alongside the edge of a river. Leti soaks it all in, "I could totally see myself living here. Look at all this beauty. Now this is somewhere you want to retire to..."

They pause to observe two small gravestones by the river.

Leti pauses, "Oh".

Aaron answers, "Yeah, maybe not..."

Aaron scrapes away moss to reveal carvings that read: 'Esther Burnley, 1812-1817. Percival Burnley, 1814-1817'.

Leti calculates their ages, "...So young. 3 and 5... How awful".

"They must've drowned in this river".

They hear a woman squealing from behind the chapel...

In Bryan's twin room, Rob sits at the desk and works on his laptop. He edits a website that reads 'Shay's Spirit Tourists'. Bryan peers over Rob's shoulder, "I'm hittin' the bar. You coming?".

Rob declines, "Nah. I'll join ya later".
"Workaholic!"
"Alcoholic!"
"Touché"

 At the hotel bar, Shay and Deborah sip from elegant glasses filled with expensive wine. Bryan joins them and sits on a bar stool.
Shay asks, "Where's Rob?"
Bryan answers, "Seems like he can't take orders".
Deborah sighs, "Trying to make a good impression?"
Shay slurs, "Well he can't elbow his way in. Takes a lifetime to build an empire like we have... I'm always suspicious of outsiders..."
A Bartender approaches, "What can I get you, sir?"
Bryan orders, "Double Scotch on the rocks".
The Bartender asks, "We have a wide array of whisky. What tickles your fancy?"
Bryan inquires, "Oooh, do you have Laphroaig?"
The Bartender smiles, impressed he would select Islay whisky, a connoisseur's drink, "Excellent choice, sir. Coming right up. Thank God you didn't order Jack Daniels. You are clearly a man of taste".
The bartender prepares the drink.
Bryan admires the bar, "This place is something else".
Shay boasts, "Oh, you ain't seen nothin' yet..."

 Outside, behind the chapel, Aaron and Leti reach the area where the woman's squeal was coming from. They discover a Groundskeeper and a Group of Hotel Guests huddling in the darkness as they wield sonar equipment... Aaron and Leti glance at one another with raised eyebrows, wondering what on Earth they have just interrupted...
The groundskeeper motions for Leti and Aaron to stay quiet and hands them equipment, as if they were latecomers to the group. They put their headphones on. Aaron and Leti listen to the sonar sounds of strange noises...

 To their amazement, bats flutter and flap around the group. Aaron and Leti observe the bats in awe. The bats encircle the chapel steeple.

Bats even skim across the river and fly past the gravestones...

  Meanwhile, Rob works on editing software on his laptop in his room. He begins a fancy edited trailer for Shay's paranormal investigation website. The lamp flickers. Rob hears an old door creak open. Rob stops editing, turns and peers into the shadows, "Bryan? You're back early..."
No answer.
Rob turns in his seat, "That you, mate?".
No answer.
Rob rises from the chair quietly and clenches his fists, as if he is about to be attacked by an intruder. Rob tiptoes across the floorboards. He discovers the main door is closed shut. Rob checks that the lock chain is still hooked.
It is.
He peers through the peep hole into the empty corridor.
Nothing is on the other side but carpet and wall.
Rob appears confused. He checks the bathroom door, opens and closes it and listens for a creak...
Nothing.
Rob searches the room for another door. He runs his hand along the aged wallpaper. Rob discovers a bump behind the wallpaper in the shape of an old doorframe. Rob leans closer. The unfinished trailer suddenly plays on Rob's laptop loudly. Rob rushes to pause the video.
What the--
Rob's phone vibrates on the counter and makes him jump.
Fuck me!
Rob grabs his phone, checks the text message, glances at his watch, closes the laptop and leaves, deciding that heading for dinner with the rest of the group is a safer bet right now, rather than be left alone in this creepy room all night. The empty room seems to settle...

...Then, the sound of an old door creaks open again...

Unseen footsteps walk around the room. The laptop is pushed off the table by an unseen force.

Shay, Deborah, Bryan, Aaron, Leti and Rob enter a grand, private dining hall with their wine glasses. An old oak table set with fine plates and silverware stretches across the room. Exquisite furnishings surround it. Shay sits at the head of the candlelit table. Deborah and Bryan sit at his side. Leti and Aaron sit opposite each other. Rob sits last, opposite Shay.

Rob apologises, "Sorry I'm late".

Shay complains, "What did I say about a 'no work' policy?"

Deborah states, "Won't get you any further, try as you might".

Bryan calms, "Go easy on him, he's new. He'll learn".

Rob jokes, "Well a bit of work won't kill me, will it?".

Shay stands, taps a spoon on his wine glass and then raises his it. Shay asks, "What do you think, eh? Grand enough for 'Shay's Spirit Tourists'? Who says I don't treat my team well, huh? This place is fit for a King and Queen—"

Shay tips his glass in the direction of himself and Deborah.

"...Prince and Princess—"

Shay gestures towards Aaron and Leti.

"...Knight and... Erm... Pauper".

Shay points at Bryan and Rob.

He continues his speech, "Soak it all in. You've earned it. Helped me build this company from the ground up. Who would have imagined we'd have come this far? Back then we were younger and slimmer, investigating people's basements, discovering only their rickety pipes. Travelling the country, seeking to exploit any opportunity for paranormal activity. Now look at us. IN ENGLAND! Drink wine, dine and be merry! Spirit Tourists, I salute you".

They each clink their glasses together across the table in a toast.

"To us!"

"Enjoy!".

"The night is young".

"Cheers".

They gulp alcohol. Waiters and Waitresses bring dinner in on silver platters. They serve delicious food and leave. The group relaxes at the table. Aaron, worse for wear after plenty of wine, picks a fight...

Aaron states, "I'm not buying it".

Shay grins, "Good 'cos I ain't sellin' it".

"What you hiding?"

"Aaron, dear nephew, ever the cynical skeptic. Show some gratitude, for once, your Uncle's footing the bill".

"That's exactly my point. Since when do you pay for anything? It's all been about you getting paid lately..."

"There's a first for everything, dear boy. A reward for your hard work. Eat. Take the night off. Lessen your paranoia... There will be plenty of chances for that as our trip continues and we get to work..."

The group tucks into dinner.

Bryan, ever the pacifist, changes the subject to ease the growing tensions, " I'd read about these mansions but nothing prepared me for this. It's on a whole new level".

Leti beams, "You seen our room? I just wish we were getting married in it or something..."

Aaron jests, "Scares the shit outta me".

"Marriage?"

"No, the whole medieval history vibe in there. Could take out an army with the weapons on the walls! I hope they're replicas".

Deborah puts on her channeling voice, "Ohhhh, Aaron. They're not replicas. I am sensing that those weapons have ended lives. I can see it in their aura".

Leti seems shocked, "That's barbaric".

Shay suggests, "We'll gladly switch rooms if you can't handle it".

Leti claims, "Oh, I can handle it. These English are a bit sick, don't you think?"

Rob interrupts, "Easy on the racism, love. Don't forget whose country you're in".

Leti continues, "Why have them on display though? If they're war relics. I mean they've KILLED PEOPLE!".

Bryan informs, "Oh, it's like it all over the land. You can view the dress Mary Queen of Scots was executed in. There's still blood on the collar! And the guillotine blade that beheaded Marie Antoinette".

Shay slices into his rare steak. Blood oozes out.

Shay jokes, "It's the torture equipment that gives me a kick. Eurgh!".

Bryan explains, "All this living history is perfect for us. I can't wait to get stuck into a good séance or Ouija session. Just imagine the results. The activity should be phenomenal. I'm expecting big things".

Aaron muses, "Must fuck with the Brits' heads".

Rob suddenly points a knife at Aaron, which shocks the group.

Rob growls, "That's why your ancestors left... They couldn't stick it. Gotta be tough to live here".

Eventually, he lowers the knife. The group takes it as a bad joke. Much later, having eaten their meals, Deborah slaps Shay's full belly. Clean plates and empty wine glasses bring dinner to a close. Shay struggles out of his seat as the buttons of his shirt burst at the seams. Deborah helps him up, "Better get this beast to bed before they do us for indecent exposure".

Shay slaps Deborah's ass, "So that's what's on your mind, eh?"

Shay and Deborah make their way through an eerily quiet corridor to their room. They stifle laughter as drunken steps prove more difficult. Lights flicker as Rob and Bryan cross a separate corridor. Elsewhere, Leti gets anxious as she feels like something unseen follows her. She hurries along the corridor to Aaron. Unbeknownst to Leti, her scarf is pulled from out of her handbag. Aaron reaches their door and Leti clings to him. Aaron spots the scarf on the carpet down the hallway. "That yours, babe?"

Leti checks her handbag in fear.

"Yes... What the hell? I tucked that deep down... You get it. Please".

Aaron makes the sound of a ghost, "Ooooooooh".

"I'm not joking".

Aaron creeps along the corridor. Leti views a painting that hangs on its own on the wall. It features a beautiful woman with striking resemblance to Leti, along with written words that read: 'Lady Lloyd. 1665'. Aaron wraps the scarf around his neck like a noose. Leti turns to Aaron who pretends to hang himself.

"Stop messing about. Come here".

Aaron drops to the floor and seems to slide backwards down the hall. Leti shrieks. Aaron finishes the trick by doing 'the worm' dance move. He hurries to his feet and chuckles.

"Idiot. You'll wake the neighbours".

"I'm not the one screaming".

Aaron stumbles into the bedroom and Leti locks the door. He views the uncomfortable camping bed with disdain, "Change your mind about the sleeping arrangements yet?"

"Ahhh, so that was your plan all along?"

"Get you scared enough that you want to cosy up to me? Sure..."

"Nah, I'm not that desperate yet. Will take more than that."

"Is that a challenge?"

"Don't you dare"

"Damn, I clearly didn't scare you enough".

Leti pulls her family history scrapbook out and scribbles a note that reads: 'Lady Lloyd, 1665?'. She heads for the bathroom and undresses on the move. She seductively glances over her shoulder and closes the bathroom door. Aaron listens to the bath taps run water. He grins.

In their own room, Deborah and Shay snuggle and giggle in bed under the covers.

Shay teases, "Time to show you who's a beast".

Deborah yawns, "Believe me, I already know".

Elsewhere, Bryan snores in bed. Rob picks up his laptop from the floor, confused as to how it got there. He assumes Bryan was trying to make a 'no work policy' point. Rob plugs in headphones as he edits more of the Spirit Tourist website in the dark...

The lamp flickers. Rob stares at it.

Goddamn faulty wiring... They need to sort out the electrics in this joint.

A pillow hits Rob in the head and makes him jump. But he discovers, thankfully, that it was Bryan who threw it, "Go to sleep".

Rob shuts off his laptop, turns off the lamp and gets in bed.

In their stunning bathroom, Leti eases into the bubble bath and relaxes. Hot steam rushes into the cold air outside through an open bathroom window. Leti closes her eyes and enjoys her bath. In their main bedroom, Aaron reads a book in his boxer shorts and tries to get comfy on the squeaky, camper bed. In the bathroom, Leti's eyes open as she hears what she thinks sounds like children crying in the distance. Her mind goes straight to those two gravestones by the river. She sees a flash of the memory of witnessing them in her mind's eye. The sounds of crying grow louder. Leti sits up with concern. In the bedroom, Aaron snoozes on the camper bed with the book on his chest. If it had not been such a long flight and bus trip, he would not have been able to fall asleep so quickly on so uncomfortable a bed. The shrill cries of Leti in the bathroom wake Aaron.

Aaron rushes into the bathroom in his boxers. He relaxes when he discovers that Leti is safe. She covers her dignity as he strides to the window and peers outside. Leti observes with worry. Aaron chuckles. Leti ask, "What is that noise? Scares the hell outta me".
Aaron answers, "They're Peacocks. Must be their mating call or something... God, it sounds like children crying."
"What a relief, I thought it was-- Hey, get out you perv".
Leti splashes Aaron with bath water.
"You were just playing Knight in shining armour to cop an eyeful. Shame on you".
Aaron leaves the bathroom. Leti closes the bathroom window.

Later, Leti enters the bedroom in a bath robe. Aaron lies on the four poster bed dressed in the full suit of armour from the wall.
Leti laughs, "You've got some nerve".
Aaron flicks up the helmet visor to reveal a massive grin.
"I'm just surprised it fits".
"Especially your big head".
"Can you help me out of it? I think I'm stuck..."
Leti slams the visor down.

Outside, a full moon shines across the Gothic mansion estate.

Peacocks sleep in the gardens. Bats hang upside down from the chapel roof. The river rushes past the children's graves.

Leti sleeps in the four-poster bed alone. The bedsheets wrap tightly around her. The four-poster creaks. Pressure applies to the bottom of the duvet as someone climbs onto the bed. Leti awakes from her slumber with her eyes closed, "Aaron, get off. I'm not afraid of peacocks". The movement continues up the duvet, she complains "I won't warn you again. Get back to your own bed now".

Then, Leti hears Aaron snore from his own camper bed. Leti's eyes bolt open. She turns over. Leti screams as the large silhouette of a man straddles her. Aaron leaps out of bed, ready to fight, and crashes into the suit of armour he had cast aside earlier. Leti throws a pillow at the apparition which disappears just as Aaron turns the light on.
"The fuck was that?"
"I thought it was you. Then I heard you snoring".

The room is empty.

"Did you see it, Aaron?"
"I don't know, I was just coming out of an intense nightmare..."

Damp spots cover the duvet. Leti is as white as the sheets.
She gives in, "Come here".
"Huh?"
"Get in bed with me NOW".
"You've changed your tune, Leti".
"'Cos now I'm scared..."

Leti throws open the duvet covers, "You coming in before I change my mind?".
Aaron charges, stubbing his toe by mistake on the suit of armour, and painfully leaps into the four-poster with Leti.
Leti complains, "I'm wet. So is the bed".
Aaron jokes, " I have that effect on most women".

Leti slaps Aaron playfully.

"Chill, babe, you just had a nightmare is all. Wow, you are sweaty".

Leti points at a halberd on the wall, "Bust a move or try anything and I'll skewer you with that".

Aaron views the halberd with despair, turns off the light and snuggles up to Leti. She asks, "What's poking me?"

Aaron jokes, "A weapon of my own".

"Ew! Get your boner off me!"

"It'll keep you warm".

"Right, I'm fetching the halberd"

Leti slaps Aaron's boner under the covers.

"Ouch! Preferred you when you were a wailing banshee".

"I'll make you scream like one if you put that thing near me again".

Aaron turns onto his back. The duvet covers rise because of his hard-on. He nudges Leti, "Look, there's a ghost beneath the bedsheets". She can't help but laugh but still she threatens, "Get back in that camper bed".

"Ok, ok, I'll knock it off"

"You won't do anything to that thing. Quit the innuendos!"

"Good night..."

"Mmm-hmm... We'll see about that".

Meanwhile, Bryan and Rob snore in their twin room. The sound of an old door creaks open. The sounds of children giggling and whispering as footsteps patter across the carpet. This is definitely not a couple of peacocks... The sound of an old door slams and wakes Bryan. Thinking he was just dreaming, he drifts back to sleep.

Elsewhere, Shay and Deborah sleep in their double bed. The silhouette of the man who leapt on Leti's bed stands at the foot of their bed... Watching... Staring... Glaring...

The next morning, the Sun rises and casts an orange glow across the estate. In the hotel, Shay, Deborah, Bryan, Rob, Aaron and Leti descend the archaic stairwell with their luggage. A receptionist greets

them with a smile, "Good morning all".
"Morning".
"Did you enjoy your brief stay with us?"
"Out of this world, truly sensational, thank you".
"That's what we like to hear".

 'Shay's Spirit Tourists' hand in their individual room keys to the receptionist. The receptionist glances at Leti and Aaron, "And how about the young couple? Did you enjoy the Kingmaker's Chamber?"
Leti seems off-guard and Aaron is mid-yawn.
The Receptionist inquires, rather suspiciously, "No complaints at all? Leti dismisses, "Why? Should there be?"
"Well, that will be a record..."
"What do you mean?"
"You'll be the first guests who won't have something to report!"

Leti and Aaron glance at Shay. Shay grins, the trick up his sleeve coming into fruition...
The Receptionist, "Did they not know?".
Leti asks, losing her temper, "Know what exactly?"
"Should I tell them or will you?"
Shay hurries out, "I wanna make it out of here alive", and grabs his luggage. The receptionist hands the rest of the group a hotel flyer. A slogan reads: 'Voted the most haunted hotel in Britain.'
The Receptionist congratulates, "Most people don't make it through the night. You'd be surprised how many half-naked couples flee from that room at around 3am wanting an express check out".
Aaron laughs, "Knew it. Treat my ass. "Warned you 'bout Uncle Shay!".
Leti marches out of the hotel.
The Receptionist waves goodbye, "Have a pleasant trip".

 The group boards the tour bus. They find Shay in a seat with his hands raised as if he's about to come under attack. Deborah throws something at Shay and he laughs.
Deborah states, "Well you had me fooled".
Shay chastises, "Switch your paranormal powers on, people, from

here on in. That was my little test to see if any of you are the 'real deal'. Don't trust me when I next say " Have a night off". There are NO nights off in this trade... Not when there's money to be made!".

Aaron pulls a bucket of fire emergency sand from behind a seat and places it next to Shay. Old letters read: 'IN CASE OF FIRE'.
Aaron jokes, "That's where I'll bury my head when you start with your ghost stories", still remaining cynical.
Rob starts up the bus engine as everyone takes their seats. The exhaust expels fumes as the tour bus leaves the estate. Black diesel smoke gradually clears from the hotel front, like an eerie ghost. Something about the shape is eerily reminiscent of the intruding silhouette from the night before... It seems to follow the bus at a snail's pace...

The tour bus speeds along the motorway. Rob puffs a cigarette as thick smoke leaves the driver's window. Deborah addresses the group with excitement, "Didn't wanna put you all off last night but I felt so much activity there. You couldn't ignore it". She realizes that her reputation is at stake if she doesn't suddenly have a lot of retrospective paranormal reports at the 'most haunted hotel in the UK'...
Aaron catches on, "Come off it, Deb, you'd have brought it up immediately if you experienced anything. Nothing keeps you quiet". Rob extinguishes his cigarette butt in Aaron's sand bucket. Rob grabs his laptop from the shelf and passes it to Shay, revealing the surprise work he had been doing to impress the team.
Rob boasts, "Fruits of my labour".
Shay grabs Rob's laptop and watches, deciding the best tactic is to merely be unimpressed whatever is in store...

Deborah continues, "I'm telling you all. I heard stuff".
Leti stares outside through the bus window, keeping quiet about her own intense, actually supernatural experience.
Aaron asks, "Like what?"
Deborah answers, "Er, I heard, erm, heavy breathing".

Aaron chuckles, "That'll be Shay snoring then!".

Rob nervously demands, "Guys, enough of the bullshit, check out the trailer I made".

Shay orders, "Keep your eyes on the road, Rob. Do your actual job".

Deborah continues, "At one point, Spirit held a knife to my neck. That's why I kept so quiet. It threatened me to stay silent, you see... Didn't want to anger it. Now we're away from that accursed building, I feel safe enough to make my report. There was more too. Listen--".

Aaron rolls his eyes. Shay begins Rob's video and positions it so the rest can see. A snappy, scary trailer for 'Shay's Spirit Tourists' plays.

Rob seems proud at the wheel, "Finished it last night".

Aaron congratulates, "So, Spielberg, what did you do before we all came over to Merry 'Ole?".

Rob appears hesitant to tell that story. "Worked on pyrotechnics for a band. I'm just a collection of half-chased obsessions".

Aaron retorts, "Ah, a gadget guy. Why did you stop?".

Rob changes the subject, "What do you think of the vid?".

Shay claps the laptop shut, "It'll do. For now", and passes the laptop back to Rob.

Bryan tries to avoid another argument, "Good job, Rob. Well done".

Rob claims, "Look, I can help this company grow".

Shay explains, "We keep things simple around here. Why fix something that ain't broke?".

Leti nudges Aaron and subtly shows him a newspaper website on her phone. The article reads: 'TOUR TRAGEDY: STAGE OF TERROR'.

Aaron asks, "So, what were you saying, Rob? About what you did before and why you stopped?".

Rob coldly replies, "I wasn't".

Aaron accuses, "Says here the whole band died".

Rob turns around while driving. The bus sways and almost goes off the road, "What you reading back there?".

Shay yells, "Rob. Drive. Eyes on the road!".

Rob complains, "Why's he shit stirring? Spreading rumours?".

Aaron states, "Technology, eh? Internet's a beautiful thing".

Leti asks, "What happened to the band? How did they die?"

Rob scoffs, "Trust everything you read online?"

Aaron asks, "What shouldn't we believe, Rob?"

Rob jokes, "You're the so-called psychics, you tell me..."

Shay demands, "If you don't 'fess up now, we'll hire someone else to drive this bus..."

Rob fears losing this job, "There was an accident, ok? I'd rather not talk about it. It still hurts, you know".

Aaron reads the article aloud: "Rushed cheap labour for a charity gig was partly to blame for the stage tragedy that took the lives of all four band members."

Rob begs, "Aaron. Stop—"

Aaron continues, "Faulty pyrotechnics, dodgy electrics and poor construction resulted in a stage collapse and small explosion that ended the lives of young talent too soon."

Deborah closes her eyes and rubs the seat covers, sensing the opportunity to show off her talents, "A bearded man has just sat next to me. He wants to speak. He demands justice..."

Shay hurries for his camera and films his wife in awe, "Channel him, Deb. Do your thing..."

Deborah channels, "Ohhhhh. So full of life, pure talent; wasted. He played bass. Rock music".

Shay speaks to the camera, "We're picking up on the tragedy of an on-stage accident that took the lives of a whole band in England". He sums up the newspaper article to his audience as if this is information that has been delivered in a séance and not from an online blog.

Rob shakes his head and seems angry, witnessing the charlatans busy at work. *So this is what they're truly like behind closed doors...*

Deborah claims, "This vehicle was their home. He welcomes us as guests—"

Rob cuts their footage short, interrupting, "This was a back-up transport bus and they were a dubstep group. Something awful must've happened to a different group. Funny that... They never came on this one..."

Deborah opens her eyes, embarrassed. Shay sheepishly turns off the camera. He'll delete the footage later. *Thank God it wasn't livestream.*

Aaron asks, "How'd you survive then, Rob?"

Rob claims, "Oh, me? I was backstage".
Aaron sarcastically retorts, "Must have been a miracle..."
Rob answers, "Yeah. A miracle..."

The tour bus passes a sign on the edge of the motorway that reads: 'Welcome to Warwickshire: Shakespeare's County.'

Later, once their journey is complete and their tour bus safely parked, Shay leads his group past an ornate, Tudor building. A sign reads: 'Birthplace of William Shakespeare'.
Deborah gasps, "I can't wait to talk to good old Bill the Bard..."
Shay informs, "Hold your horses, that ain't what we're here for. Further up".
Deborah photographs a selfie outside the attraction. Bryan reads a tour guide of Stratford-Upon-Avon. Aaron and Leti amble along the street, hand-in-hand. Rob stays at the back of the group.

Shay reaches their actual destination. He stands outside a smaller Tudor building; the remains of a Coaching Inn which now features an eccentric shop front. A flyer on the front door reads: 'Join in on an evening of Spiritual activity with world-famous 'Shay's Spirit Tourists'. October 31st, 9pm-3am, tickets £30'.

Deborah, Bryan, Rob, Aaron and Leti join Shay. The Owner of the building, a fifty-year-old self-proclaimed psychic, and amateur dramatic thespian, greets the group.
"It's an honour to meet you all. Welcome to Stratford-upon-Avon. Shakespeare was not the only thing to happen here, trust me... But you'll discover that for yourselves... Come on in, make yourselves at home. Don't be shy, now". The owner leads the group inside his establishment, keen for the business these Americans will bring.

The foyer is creepy and old-fashioned. Bryan appears unnerved by what he senses in his surroundings. Shay checks his watch: 8:15pm. The owner addresses the group, "I would give you a tour myself but the less I tell you about this place the more it might surprise you".

Shay explains, "We need to get set up anyway. Not long before we begin our event".
"I'll get my things and be off then. Let me get out of your hair".
The owner heads for a back room.
Shay addresses his team, "Let's get started".
The group splits up and explores the property separately.

Leti leads Aaron up the narrow staircase. Aged, wooden floorboards creak with every footstep.
Aaron jokes, "Glad you're going first".
Leti scoffs, "You ditched your shining armour quickly".

Aaron and Leti enter a dark chamber with a sign that reads: 'Transfiguration Room'. The room features a wooden throne on an elevated platform. Various peculiar items of historical interest are on display.
Aaron reads, "Transfiguration Room. Spooky".
Leti states, "Bryan will fit in well here. You've not seen his mediumship have you?"
Aaron yawns, "There's an Oscar trophy on the bus waiting for him when I do, no doubt".
Leti laughs, "He'll open your eyes to the truth. You'll see..."

Elsewhere in the building, Deborah and Shay enter the Seance room. A Ouija board and crystal ball sit on a wooden table. Shay admires himself in the floor-to-ceiling mirrors that line the walls like wallpaper. He sucks in his belly so he looks less fat, which is an almost impossible endeavour. He quickly gives up and his gut spills over his belt.
Deborah seems excited, "We're guaranteed activity here".
Shay whispers, "I have a few tricks up my sleeve just in case".

Meanwhile, Rob reaches the third-storey corridor alone and carries a work bag. It is almost pitch black. He pops his head into a Spirit Cabinet with a chair inside. He peeks into a child's playroom and views the old toys. He rests his bag on the corridor floor.

Bryan pulls himself up and into the attic space. He searches the darkness with a flashlight. He discovers a collection of dusty antiques and a baby pram. He blows the dust off a bookcase and views the books. Bryan hears a deep, gutteral groan. He spins on his heel and scans the attic with the flashlight. He realizes the groan comes from below. It does not sound human...

Rob drills a hole into a beam of the corridor ceiling. The old oak squeaks as if it bellows with pain. Rob fixes a night vision camera in place. The owner sprints up the stairs and discovers Rob.
"What on Earth are you doing, you idiot?"
"Gettin' set-up. Whaddaya think?"
"That's 16th Century Tudor oak you're drilling into!"
The owner snatches the drill from Rob and heads downstairs.
"You'll be paying for the damage yourself..."
Bryan peeks below from the attic and views Rob with disdain.

After the brief exploration is done, and so the team is prepared for the night ahead, Shay reads an article on his phone about local ghost stories and the building's history while in the foyer. A cynic might call this cheating... Shay calls it a trick up his sleeve.

The owner descends the stairs with Rob's drill. He thrusts it into Shay's hands.
"You're already damaging the place".
"Who used that drill?"
"Your English chap".
"Oh, he's not one of us. I'll have words with him. I'm sorry".
"I won't tolerate any more damage".
Shay takes the hint, counts cash from his wallet and pays the owner for the evening's hire, "You have my word. No more damage."
The owner dramatically raises a hand to his head, "I should cancel tonight's shenanigans. Never in my life—"
Shay takes the hint and slips a few extra notes to the owner, "For your troubles".
The owner snatches the cash, hands Shay the keys and hurries out.

Meanwhile, upstairs, Rob tests a secret gadget under the table of the seance room. He pushes a button and the table vibrates and moves slightly. Rob notices one of the mirrors wobbles on its own. He assumes that the movement of the table set that off.

Condensation appears as if someone breathes on the mirror but he doesn't see it.

Shay enters the room with a fire extinguisher, "Look what I found. My gift to you". Shay throws the fire extinguisher at Rob who catches it. "Bit of a sick joke, don't you think?"
"It's a reminder. Don't fuck about. My reputation's on the line here. No more damage". Shay leaves the room. Rob views the mirror. The strange breath condensation is gone.

Later, 'Shay's Spirit Tourists' have the building to themselves. LED candlelights flicker in the foyer. The place seems like a ghostly theme park attraction due to gadgets and decorations that they have brought along with them for added effect. Deborah greets Spirit Tourists, the paying customers who gather in a huddle.
She puts on a performance voice, "Good evening all. Oh, yes, good evening. I trust you are all prepared to glimpse past the Veil that separates our world from the next. Dare to venture with us into the Void. You'll walk away changed people before the night is done. A truly unforgettable all-nighter awaits you"...
Deborah takes cash from the guests in exchange for tickets and continues, "This foyer is the safest room in the building. We'll make it a comfort space; our sanctuary".
Spirit tourists view their surroundings in excitement, eager to begin the ghost hunt and get stuck into the night ahead.
Deborah says, "Once we ascend the stairs, there's no telling what we might discover. I will have no say in that. Spirit will decide".
Deborah closes the door behind the last of the tourists. She pockets the cash and addresses the gathering from the stairs, "Now we are gathered, let me perform a cleansing ritual. Please hold hands and form a circle".

The group forms a circle and holds hands.

Deborah orders, "Close your eyes".

The group closes their eyes.

She performs her ritual, "You are all equipped to protect yourselves from the forces of darkness. If you get frightened, picture a safe zone in your mind's eye. Just go to this private place of light and you can stop anything that comes your way".

Deborah closes her eyes, raises her hands and chants. A few of the spirit tourists glance at each other, wondering what they have got themselves into.

She finishes and says, "We are ready. Spirit is willing. Follow me".

Night-vision cameras film the party as they slowly climb the stairs. Shay waits at the top of the staircase, in the dark, for dramatic effect. Deborah and the spirit tourists pause their ascent.

Shay announces, "Greetings, spirit tourists, spiritual friends, I am Spirit Master Shay. I shall be your guide into the spiritual world and open your eyes to the paranormal. You are guaranteed activity tonight. The building you have entered is steeped in gruesome history. A Tudor coaching inn, it was the largest of its kind in 16th century Stratford. These walls have absorbed so much evil, terror and pain. Does anyone feel uneasy on this staircase, by any chance? Please know, at any point tonight, if you should see, sense, smell, hear or feel anything out of the norm whatsoever, you must announce it. It is a way that Spirit lets itself be known. We all can be sensitive to this. It is a gift. Back to the stairs. Anyone feeling anything out the ordinary? Anything strange?"

A female spirit tourist raises her hand.

Deborah gasps, "Good. Thank you, Spirit. If anyone else feels anything at all throughout the night you must tell us. Simply raise your hand. Spirit has a way of communicating with us all".

Shay asks, "Pray tell, ma'am".

The female tourist explains, "My heart's racing, I feel nervous".

Deborah places her hand on the woman's belly, "How is your stomach feeling exactly?"

"It... It hurts. I don't know why".

Deborah glances at Shay.

Shay leaps into theatrical action, "SPIRIT! WELCOME! Ladies and Gentlemen, already we have a spirit among us. We are lucky to have this happen so soon... A female servant of this old inn fell pregnant by her master. In a foul rage, for fear of discovery, the master pushed her down the stairs; killing the woman and her unborn child. Now let us move on".

The spirit tourists hurry to climb the stairs, talking amongst themselves about the so-called discovery.

Bryan hangs his head as he sits in the throne of the transfiguration room. Shay and Deborah invite the tourists inside. Aaron watches Bryan from the doorway, eager to discover what Leti was teasing him about earlier. He intends to pay attention, which is out of the norm for him, usually being the most cynical one in the room.

Shay continues, "Welcome to the Transfiguration Room. Our Medium, Bryan, will communicate with the Other Side. When he enters trance, do not touch him. He will not touch you".

The electric candlelights flicker and go out. Perfectly on cue...

Deborah screams, "SILENCE! Ohhhhhh... Silence... Sweet, sweet, deathly silence... Spirit is here".

Bryan suddenly takes a deep gasp of breath, filling his lungs.

The spirit tourists move back from Bryan and the throne. Bryan hangs his head lower. Aaron grins and views the frightened audience, wondering if any of them are falling for it. *I guess this is what it takes to get people out of their houses, away from Netflix, these days. Cinema has lost its charm so people need something like this to entertain them. What has the world come to... Look at 'em... They want to believe it so they'll force themselves to fall for parlour tricks... So pathetic...*

Aaron spots a Green Man necklace on the side, admires it and pockets it, thinking nothing of the small-time theft...

Shay continues, "We are here to speak with you".

Bryan channels a spiritual entity and his voice changes dramatically. He speaks with a perfect, archaic English accent, as though it was not his own...

"How mayest I be of service to thee?".

Aaron's grin fades. He steps into the room for a closer look. *There's no way that voice is coming from him. That's too much of a change. Way too deep a pitch. He must have a microphone or a pitch changer or speakers or something... That's crazy. I'm almost impressed, if I didn't know what these guys are like...*

Shay questions, "Who am I dealing with?"
Bryan cackles like a maniac. His face begins to change in front of everyone with a pair of eyes.
Aaron leans up the wall by the throne and peers at Bryan. His face is physically changing through transfiguration in a way that would seem impossible to do yourself. *Ok, so what's the gig here then? Is there a light projection forming an illusion that's making it look like his face is actually changing? I've gotta ask 'em about this later... I'll admit, this is pretty decent...*

A male spirit tourist raises his hand and speaks up, "Father Davis?"
Bryan launches himself forward from the seat, as if about to attack the man. Aaron stops him, surprised by Bryan's aggression and strength.
"Thou mock me? What be thy title?"
Deborah and Shay display concern on their faces. Shay answers, "I am Spirit Master Shay".
Deborah states, "No-one mocks you, Spirit—"
"Silence, wench!"
Shay interrogates, "Father Davis was your name in life?".
Bryan views Shay with contempt. All of his physical features are so altered it no longer looks like Bryan. They are dealing with something else entirely...
The male spirit tourist raises his hand and speaks, "Forgive me Father for I have sinned. It's been five weeks since my last confession".
Bryan bellows with anger. Aaron restrains him.
Shay shakes his head at the spirit tourist to silence him.
"What sayest thou?"
Shay answers, "We come here with respect".

"Thou wouldst not know respect if it pillaged thee up the arse, ill-breeding varlot!".

Aaron rests Bryan back in the throne. Bryan embeds his fingernails into the wooden arms of the chair and begins to scratch deeply, breaking some of them back and bleeding... Aaron views in horror.

  Meanwhile, Shay guides the male spirit tourist into the corridor. He whispers with him, out of earshot from the rest of the group.
Shay asks, "What's with all this priest talk?".
The spirit tourist clutches a crucifix around his neck, "You and Deborah told us to speak up if we felt anything. Someone spoke the words into my head. I couldn't control my lips".
Shay rests a hand on his shoulder, "Let me take it from here. You mustn't speak. You're angering it and I don't want this to get out of hand." Shay ushers the tourist into the room but waits outside. He secretly goes on his phone. He google searches 'Stratford ghost priest' and finds an historical account.

  The article shocks Shay as he reads about a Priest who was found hiding in a priest hole covered in blood and sent to the gallows for murder. His last words were about confession.

Bryan's cackles reverberate through the house.

  Back in the room, night vision cameras capture the transfiguration as tourists gather around Bryan and the throne. Shay relieves Aaron of his duty and kneels in front of Bryan. Bryan stretches and cracks his neck muscles in an inhuman manner.
Shay asks, "May I call you Father?"
"I be no Father to thee, heathen".
Deborah bites her thumb skin nervously.
The spirit tourists gaze in fear and awe.
Shay continues, "Father Davis, I know of you".
"Thou knowest naught!"
"...You were hanged for your crimes".

Bryan roars with fury. Electric candles and other gadgets fly off the mantelpiece, "LET NOT THIS KNAVE ESCAPE!".
Shay advises, "Stay calm, guys. Spirit can't harm us".
"Thou art certain of this?"
"Spirit, you harmed enough in life, you do not frighten me in death".
Deborah interrupts, concerned for her husband, "Shay—"
Bryan immediately mimics Deborah's voice perfectly, "Shay, we're not ready. Think of our business. We can't keep the baby".

   This revelation stuns the group, especially Deborah and Shay. No-one but them knew about their abortion years ago, when they started their new company... Shay steps forward and presses his hand on Bryan's forehead. Bryan lets loose one last guttural cackle and bares rotten teeth; only a few remain. Shay whispers into Bryan's ear. Bryan spits out rotten teeth that scatter across floorboards. Bryan's head drops. He exits the trance-like state and his own features suddenly return to his face. The electric candles turn on from the floor. The teeth are nowhere to be seen. The blood and fingernails on the chair are not there and healed. Bryan speaks with his own voice again, as if totally unaware of everything that just happened.
"Good evening everyone, shall we begin?"...

   A midnight buffet lies on the side for the guests. Everyone believes that they needed a well-earned break after that unexpected experience. Aaron and Leti find a corner to themselves.
Leti boasts, "Converted yet?".
Aaron tucks into a mince pie, with his mind wrapped in thought. Leti kisses him on the cheek, knowing what he must be going through right about now.
Other Spirit Tourists eat snacks and drink port. An impressive selction of cheese is particularly being picked into.
Shay and Bryan enter the foyer. The tourists seem worried by Bryan.
Shay assures them, "Nothing to worry about guys. He's back to being plain ole Bryan. No more Father Davis, thank you very much! Enjoy your midnight snack".
Bryan advises, "We'll take a quick break. You can have some hands-on

experience for yourselves. The house is yours".

Shay states, "Help yourselves to the equipment". Shay guides Bryan out of the building. Various ghost-hunting gadgets line a separate surface. Dowsing rods, gems, Tarot cards and other devices. A few spirit tourists rush up the stairs, eager to investigate for themselves. This is the part most customers enjoy in particular. Since most people have a healthy dose of cynicism, they like to get down on hands and knees and search for hidden tricks or simply put things to the test themselves... They can play at being professional ghost hunters.

Rob follows them, eager to chase anyone of the scent should they get to close to one of his many hidden tricks.

   Shay and Bryan shiver outside in the back garden.

"You don't remember a thing?"

"Normally, I have some form of control. But this time: I was a powerless observer of myself. An out-of-body experience. Like I was viewing myself in third-person. I shudder to think what took over".

"Well you sure as hell shit me up. They're gettin' a bang for their buck, eh? This one will go viral, that's for sure..."

"Shay, something foul is here to play".

"...Excellent".

"Don't seem so excited".

   Shay gets serious for a moment, "But how did you know about our—Look. Deborah's upset".

Bryan answers guiltily, "That's what concerns me the most. I didn't know anything about that personally. But whatever took over sure did... It knew every secret about all those gathered in the room".

Shay disappears into the building. Bryan sparks up a cigarette. He observes the exterior of the Tudor building from outside and spots something above.

A Priest stares down at Bryan from a window.

   Bryan drops his cigarette. He picks it up and glances up again. A spirit tourist waves at Bryan from the same window.

Bryan takes a long drag from the cig, hands shaking, "This fuckin' place is messing with my head".

Meanwhile, a group of spirit tourists gather around the Ouija board. The mirrors show their reflections. Rob sits in the corner of the room to observe. The Ouija board planchette spells out the word: 'MURDER'. The spirit tourists appear amazed. Rob presses a button. The table vibrates and moves and terrifies the tourists. They run out of the room. Rob grins as he removes the device from beneath the table.

Rob spots a Priest covered in blood in the mirror behind him.

Rob turns and finds nothing there. He pockets his device and finds his own hands to be bloody. He scrunches his eyes and looks again: His hands are clean. *Time to stay clear of the coffee... Did they spike our drinks or lace our food? I'm hallucinating over here...*

Rob leaves the seance room. Quiet cackles from the unseen priest echo through the room after he has left. They sound exactly like the voice that Bryan spoke with while transfigured.

In the corridor, Rob hurries past the spirit cabinet and descends the stairs. The corridor is empty and dark. The curtain of the spirit cabinet moves slightly. Voices of a confession emanate from the spirit cabinet. *Goddamn it, where did the others go? Join them fast. This place is creepy as shit... Not a good house to be in alone...*

A clock in the attic ticks to 1:13. Shay climbs into the attic. Bryan follows. Spirit tourists clamber into the attic and get freaked out by the baby pram and other peculiar items. Aaron and Leti enter. Rob pops his head into the attic space.
Shay shakes his head, "Full here. Go with the others".
Rob disappears and his footsteps creak away. Leti sits on a panel that moves. *What the--* Leti moves and Aaron lifts the panel to reveal a priest hole. The walls of the hole are stained with dry blood.
Aaron gasps, "Oh fuck no".

Leti screams, "Get me outta here".
Shay requests, "Leti, wait. Aaron, close that up".
Aaron places the panel over the priest hole.
A female tourist asks, "Oh my God, what's that smell?"
A male tourist answers, "Cherry tobacco".
Leti declares, "I don't smell anything".
"It's over here".

Spirit tourists move away from the smell. Aaron's face twitches.
Bryan warns, "Something's not right".
Shay orders, "Stay calm everyone".
The female spirit tourist screams, DID YOU JUST TOUCH ME?".
"No".
Shay asks, "Spirit? Do you wish to speak?".
Aaron's face snarls into a devilish grimace. His nose creases and upper
lip shivers but remains unnoticed by the others. It seems as though
even he is unaware of it.

The priest hole cover moves slightly...

"Holy fuck".
"Wrong choice of words".

Aaron's face transfigures into old, evil, wrinkled features. Bryan
notices, "Aaron? You ok over there?".
Aaron lashes out at Leti in an unprovoked and fiercely aggressive
attack. Leti screams. Bryan and Shay separate them. Bryan covers
Aaron's eyes and chants into his ears as he guides Aaron out of the
attic. Bryan guides him through the corridor. The spirit cabinet
curtains tear open, as if ready to hear a confession.
Aaron speaks with the Priest's voice, "We meet again, Bryan". Night
vision cameras record them as Bryan guides Aaron down the stairs.
Aaron resists. Bryan struggles to move him.

Meanwhile in the attic, Shay calms the group. Leti hyperventilates.
She takes puffs from her inhaler.

Shay explains, "Bryan will protect Aaron. He'll bring him back to himself... That was out of character".
A tourist asks, "Who'll protect us?"
"He'll get him outside safely".
"Maybe that's what spirit wanted".
"All is fine. Everything is under control. They can't hurt us".
"Tell that to your friend. She looks pretty hurt to me".
"There's that smell again. Cherry tobacco".

The priest hole cover slides open... Everyone screams.

 Outside, lamps flicker along the cobbled, Tudor Stratford streets. Bryan guides Aaron out of the building and uncovers his eyes. Aaron's voice morphs from the Priest's back to his own. Something about getting him out of the building and into fresh air seems to help.
Aaron seems surprised, "Woah. What we doing out here? It's cold."
Bryan lights two cigarettes and passes one to Aaron.
"We overstepped the mark coming here".
"Eh?"
"We've bitten off more than we can chew"
"What do you mean?"
 "Aaron... You attacked Leti".
"WHAT?! I don't have an abusive bone in my body".
"I know... Something was invading your soul, latching on, taking over your body temporarily. It couldn't lash out through me but you're new to all of this so it seemed to try to with you".
"Is she ok? Did I hurt her bad?"
"We separated you".
"Oh my God".
"Still a skeptic?"
"Well, I'm not goin' back in there. What does that tell you?"
"I'd advise you not to. Had to sever the link and get you out. I don't even want to go back in there with what happened to me earlier".
Aaron takes deep drags from the cigarette, "I don't even smoke. Did I hit her?"
"This place is truly demonic".

They hear Leti scream from inside the building. Bryan sprints inside. Meanwhile, Leti, Shay and the other tourists descend the stairs. Bryan ascends and they meet in the middle, "What happened?"
Leti seems chilled to the core, "Something groped me".
Something else frightens the female tourist at the top of the stairs, at the back of the group, "GUYS! Something's pushing me down the stairs, HELP!".
Bryan yells, "Get down now".
The group hurries down the staircase. Something pushes the woman and she almost falls down the stairs. A male tourist catches her.

Deborah waits in the foyer as the group funnels in from the stairs. She turns the main lights on. People try to leave the event.
Deborah calls, "Wait, I must cleanse you. This is our sanctuary, remember?"
A male tourist scoffs, "Fuck that, I'm outta here".
Footsteps above the foyer stop the tourists in their step.
Deborah asks, "Who's did you leave behind?".
Shay, Deborah, Leti, Bryan and Rob count the group. All are accounted for.
Shay clears his throat, "Ok, guys, get together".
The main lights flicker.
Deborah demands, "Hold hands".
The group obeys.
Deborah performs her closing ritual, "As we draw this evening to a close, we gate off the Other Side and protect ourselves with light. Close your eyes".
The spirit tourists hesitate.
"Close them".
The spirit tourists obey.

The sound of a chair drags across the floorboards upstairs.

Deborah says, "Picture yourselves in a safe zone. With powers combined in our protective circle we heal ourselves and ward off evil".
A tourist asks, "Are we done? Tell me we're done".

Deborah explains, "As we leave this building, nothing will follow us from this place. The process is complete".
The spirit tourists break holding hands with their sweaty palms.

The chair from the spirit cabinet flies down the staircase and into the foyer, almost hitting the group.

The spirit tourists scream and everyone flees the building. They make their way up the cobbled street.
Deborah bids them farewell, "Travel safely now, we hope you enjoyed your spirit tour".
Shay counts cash and splits it between the group. He pockets the larger wad for himself and pays Bryan and Deborah.
Shay boasts, "That'll keep 'em talkin' for months. Great job everyone".
Shay pays Leti and Aaron, "Knew you were a natural, Aaron. You'll make the next event a sell-out. Keep it up".
Aaron tries to comfort Leti but she moves away, scared by him.
Shay gives the least amount of money to Rob. "I'm taking damages from your cut. You and your damned drill".
Shay claps his hands together, speaks to the group and rubs off the cold, "Now who's goin' back in there for our coats and kit?"...
No-one volunteers...

part two

Street lamps turn off as the Sun rises over Stratford-upon-Avon. It is a fine morning, oblivious to what occurred at night in the old Tudor Coaching Inn. Shay, Deborah, Bryan, Rob, Aaron and Leti approach the tour bus in the car park dressed in their coats as they carry their equipment. Rob had drawn the short straw to go and retrieve their belongings from the house, though he made sure to wait until daybreak, feeling like it was safer to do it during daylight...

Leti boards the tour bus. She grabs the bucket of sand and empties it over Aaron's head. He wipes sand out of his hair, picks a cigarette butt out of his ear and throws it at Rob. Later, the tour bus travels along a motorway. Bryan works on Rob's laptop on the tour bus. He downloads footage from the various night vision cameras at his side. Shay leans back and grins at Aaron.
"Still a skeptic? Told you it ran in the blood, nephew..."
Leti leaves her seat and moves to one away from Aaron. Bryan views a freeze frame from the attic footage. He hands the laptop to Deborah.
"Deb, in all my years doing this, I've never seen anything like this".
Deborah seems horrified and passes it to Shay, "Great for marketing".
Leti scolds, "I'm glad all your priorities are in order. Don't mind me getting assaulted and groped".
Deborah gasps, "You weren't acting?"
Leti storms to the tour bus toilet and locks herself inside.
"Guess I'll take that as a no... Thought that was part of the show".
Aaron muses, "There must be some rational explanation. Grandad used to talk about recordings in the rock. Seismology or something. That certain events are so highly energized that they get recorded by nature and simply loop through time".
Shay sarcastically replies, "Yeah, sure, that sounds *rational*".
Bryan states, "That might explain movements of inanimate objects or strange sightings but not literal transfiguration or dialogue in communication..."
Shay passes the laptop to Aaron who views the footage. The screen shows Aaron's face as it morphs into an old man's hideous features.
Shay calmly utters, "Rocks don't do that... Welcome to the team."
The tour bus bounces along a country road.

That night, after a long journey, Rob drives into darkness. His eyes grow weary and sleepy, thanks to last night's all-nighter and driving all day. Aaron stares at the Green Man necklace that he stole from the Tudor building, regretting that he ever took it from that Godforsaken place. The rest of the crew sleeps on the bus.

The tour bus turns onto the grounds of an abandoned Church and comes to a halt. Rob bangs the SATNAV as it malfunctions. He hops off the tour bus and views his surroundings. *Well, this ain't what I put in. Where in the fuck are we?*

The bus headlights reveal a dilapidated Church that hides behind mist and sits in the middle of nowhere. The crew wakes up as Rob boards the bus, confused.
Shay asks, "We here?"
Rob retorts, "Does it look like it? SATNAV took us way off course".
Deborah finds the Church on a digital map on her phone. She informs, "We're 20 miles away from the Victorian Institute".
Bryan comes behind Aaron and snatches the Green Man necklace. He seems furious, "WHERE DID YOU GET THIS?!".
Aaron answers, "That Tudor house".
Bryan yells, "AND YOU WERE STUPID ENOUGH TO STEAL IT?"
Bryan hurries past the crew and out of the bus. He throws the Green Man necklace into the bushes. He boards the tour bus and asks, "Does anyone else have anything from that damned building?".
The group shakes their heads.
Bryan pulls the bus door shut and locks it, "We've been led astray. Get us away from this place. There is a reason it has brought us here and I definitely do not want to find out why!".
Rob struggles to start the tour bus. The engine turns over... The headlights flicker. Shay moves Rob out of the driver seat. Deborah grabs the dodgy SATNAV and throws it out of the window too. Leti shrieks as she spots something in front of the bus.

The priest stands in drenched and bloodstained garbs in the headlights. He holds a dead girl in his arms and grins.

The headlights flicker off.
Leti squeals, "You all saw that right?".
Shay turns the key several times and the engine finally starts.

The headlights turn on: the priest is nowhere to be seen.

The Green Man necklace hurtles through the air and hits the bus
windscreen, as if something hurled it at them from the bush.

Everyone on board screams! Diesel fumes expel from the exhaust. The
tour bus skids in the mud as it makes its frantic getaway. The tour bus
bursts through a locked gate to escape. Shay howls with laughter as
he drives the tour bus, "Wooooooohoooooo! Always wanted to do
that!".
Bryan struggles back to his seat, "Cleansing rituals won't work if you
keep stolen trinkets hidden. Look at how that's affected us! Bunch of
amateurs. Be more alert next time. This can have serious
consequences. It's not child's play!".
Bryan sits behind Shay and meditates a protection spell. Leti sits by
Aaron's side and cries into his arms, "I came here to communicate
with my ancestors and spirits are tormenting me".
"Calm down, babe, you're safe now".
Aaron goes to his backpack and pulls out a notebook.
"I wasn't always a skeptic you know..."
Leti wipes away her tears. Aaron flicks to a page.
"When I was younger it was the only way I could stop my visions. To
teach myself not to believe. I wrote a poem, you'll think I'm mad now".
"No. Go on".
Aaron reads his handwritten poem:

"That man that I have always seen,
Has walked with me again in dream,
Not real, I know, but still he's free;
I can feel him freezing me.

Mind's eye will see what cannot be,
As it was dark and not worldly,
Although it slipped from memory,
His face can never be unseen.

It's Hell on Earth or so we're told,
Of deathly spirits from days of old,
And none on Earth can walk by bold,
When icy hands grasp, gripping cold.

My old beliefs I did review,
Forget dark past, create the new,
But sight of man begs questions too,
What are we, ourselves, to do?

But we'll see what we see really,
And real he stands by you and me,
And we now learn that, honestly,
He lives inside both you and me".

  Leti gulps, partially terrified by what her boyfriend just revealed to
her. The tour bus rolls onto a bumpy, narrow, country road. Shay
drives as Deborah checks the map on her phone, "Should be around
here somewhere".
Shay peers into the darkness as woodland overgrowth surrounds the
bus. Branches scrape the roof. Bushes scrape the sides. Shay stops the
bus, "Gear up, guys. I'm not having scratches on my face".
Shay hops off the tour bus with a backpack. He shines a flashlight at
the side of the bus and checks the airbrush painting of himself. Shay is
relieved as the painting of his face is unscathed.

  The crew disembarks the bus with their gear. They turn flashlights
on, carry backpacks and make their way up the beaten path.
Leti asks, "After everything we've been through, should we really be
doing another ghost hunt right about now?".
Shay orders, "New subscribers are waiting. We always need content".

Rob pulls Shay to the side for privacy, "I don't want this to be the end". Shay asks, "What are you talking about?"
"Let me come back to America with you. I can be of service. Work the website. Handle PR".
"Come off it".
"I'm serious".
"So am I".
"You'll regret it".

Shay puts his arm around Rob as they walk on, "Look, Rob, you've been great. You've shown us your country, been our tour guide. But your path ends here".
Shay marches on. Rob grimaces in the darkness.

The group crosses a field as wind howls across the meadow. Their flashlights struggle to illuminate anything at all as the darkness and thick mist swallows all light. A powerful flashlight beams into Shay's face and blinds him. The light scans the faces of the other group members. They shield their eyes with their hands.
Shay yells into the darkness, "Who's out there?"
The flashlight gets closer.
Aaron yells, "Show yourself!".

The Institute Caretaker, mid-sixties, shines his flashlight on himself from below and pulls a face. He puts on a spooky ghost voice, "Yoooooouuuuu'rrrrrreeeee laaaaaaatttttteeeee. Hee-hee-hee".
The group sighs and breathes relief. *Phew.*
Shay admits, "We got lost on the road".
The caretaker shines the flashlight in Shay's face, "Have you no respect for the dead, young man?"
Shay adds, "We'll have no sight left if you keep shining that in our eyes, let alone respect. What do you mean?".
"Well, it's not very often that people get here through the graveyard".
The caretaker illuminates an expansive burial site with old gravestones that stick out from all angles of the field. Leti hurries ahead in fear.
The Caretaker laughs, "*Now* you hurry... Watch your step".

The caretaker's flashlight reveals a path through the graves. He casts light on the imposing, Victorian Institute ahead. The group eventually reaches the frightening building. Aaron takes note of a sign in the porch that reads: 'This building was used as an Auxiliary Hospital during the Great War 1914-1918. In loving memory of the honoured dead.' A list of deceased soldiers' names and ranks rests below. Aaron says, "They're never nice places, are they? Why can't we ever visit haunted pet shops or theme parks or something?".

The caretaker pushes past Aaron with an old set of keys, "Show some respect to our dead. You already trampled their final resting places". The caretaker unlocks the heavy oak door, "I'll restart the generator. Switched it off 'cos you're an hour late. I'll be back in the morning". The caretaker hands the keys to Rob in subtle exchange for a wad of cash. The caretaker pockets the money and leaves.

Rob says, "Shay treated us at the start. Let me return the favour before you go home". Rob pushes the oak door open and shines a flashlight inside. The large, Victorian foyer is pitch black. A corridor stretches into darkness and a staircase leads up to a second floor. Another leads down to the cellar tunnels.

Rob, Shay, Deborah, Aaron, Leti and Bryan enter with their flashlights. They seem on edge.

Leti sighs, "Creepy mansion all to ourselves and the power has to be out, doesn't it..."

Deborah gasps, "This place is absolutely huge".

Shay suggests, "Let's split up and scout it out".

Aaron moans, "Yeah, great idea... Splitting up always goes well".

Bryan mentions, "Not long 'til our spirit tourists show up".

Shay admits, "Will be hard-pushed to deliver with the hype from our last tour. But paying customers are paying customers. The show must go on! I want everyone on top form tonight... It's our final send-off from Merry Ole England... Let's go BIG".

Deborah adds, "Judging this place, I'm not worried about that".

Shay orders, "Pair up".

Shay and Deborah head downstairs. Aaron and Leti head upstairs.

Rob and Bryan search the corridor.

Rob admits, "Glad I got you. You're the only one who seems to handle himself well with this stuff".

Bryan gulps, "Wouldn't be so sure of that yet".

Aaron and Leti enter a second-floor room. They discover with their flashlights, in the centre, a Victorian, horse-drawn carriage: a wooden hearse. Aaron gasps, "No way".

Leti whines, "Of allllllll the things to find".

"It's a hearse".

"Can't be real".

"This place has been changed into a museum, of course its real".

Aaron edges towards the exhibit and reads an historical information sign. He backs away, "When they said Institute, I was expectin' an insane asylum. Would rather be in one of those now".

"Speak for yourself..."

Elsewhere, Rob and Bryan thrust their flashlights into a room before they dare to peek inside. They discover a bar and a billiards table and breathe relief. Rob picks up a cue and breaks the triangle of billiard balls, "Looks like the others drew the short straw for once".

Bryan sniffs at the air, "Wouldn't be so sure of that either. Smell that?"

"Cigar smoke?"

"Cherry tobacco?"

"Think the spirits ignore the smoking ban?"

Meanwhile, Shay and Deborah work their way down a narrow, stone staircase. They shine flashlights to lead the way.

Deborah says, "Gah, I hate cellars".

"Will be great down here later..."

"Hmmm..."

Shay and Deborah peer into the darkness of the dusty cellar tunnels. The ceilings are low so they have to crouch. They hear a horrendous groan. Deborah grabs Shay in fear. Water pipes gurgle and power surges through the building. Lights on the staircase flicker on. Shay and Deborah chuckle. "Caretaker found the generator then".

"That's the first time I've seen you jump in a long while".
"Tell no-one. I have an image to maintain..."

The main lights illuminate Victorian decorations of grandeur. The group has returned together after their initial scout to prepare for the soon-to-be-arriving guests. They unpack gadgets from their backpacks in the foyer.
Aaron admits, "Victorians really creep me out".
Bryan asks, "Gas lamps? Cobbled streets? What's not to love?"
Aaron relays, "I read about this famous 16th Century Lord and Lady who were buried near here. The Victorians were fascinated with all things macabre, so bore little holes in the bottom of their lead coffins. They knew the couple had been embalmed you see. Centuries had passed since they were buried so they must've stunk to high heaven. People travelled far and wide to visit 'em. Even had tour guides. You'll never guess what they were travelling for... Those sick-fuck Victorians were actually TASTING THEM... You can look it up if you don't believe me. They'd poke sticks inside, through the holes at the bottom of those lead coffins, and would retrieve them, observe the gooey fluids, sniff the mess then lick it up! How disgusting is that? And we think we have issues in this day and age! They were licking mummy remains".

Rob carries equipment and heads for the cellar stairs, "You lot are no different. Digging into where you don't belong".
Shay says, "Ignore him. He's salty that we're not employing him full-time..."
Leti jokes, "Well I ain't suckin' corpse juice any time soon".
Shay checks his watch, "We don't have long. They'll be here any minute. Get set up. Final checks. Then double checks. I want us to go out with a bang".
Aaron admits, "I'll be glad to get out of this fucked up country".
Rob shouts from the cellar stairs, "I heard that, yank!".

Later, the foyer lights are dim and make the place look creepy. Shay addresses the group of fresh Spirit Tourist guests from the staircase. His crew stands at his side.

Shay performs, "Welcome, spirit tourists, I am Spirit Master Shay. My colleagues have scouted out the building tonight and have found the place to be extremely active. You are ready for a real treat. Ready yourselves for a paranormal adventure and put on your brave faces. This is our grand finale before we head home".

The tourists applaud and cheer. The sounds echo through the empty, cavernous hallways ominously... As if such pleasant sounds have not been heard here in a very long time... Positive emotions do not even feel acceptable in such a place.

Shay continues, "For the more courageous among you, we recommend the cellars-- We'll call them the 'tombs' tonight".

The tourists glance at one another with nervous anticipation.

Shay advises, "This place is huge, so we'll split into groups to get the most out of the evening. You'll each have 2 team members to keep you safe".

Shay divides the tourists into three groups: with himself and Deborah, Aaron and Leti, Bryan and Rob.

"Any trouble and we meet in the foyer. Happy ghost hunting!".

Bryan and Rob lead their group into a chapel. An electronic imaging device and a radio rest on a table with a chair. The device illuminates the room with green dots. The radio flicks through channels every five seconds.

Rob yawns, "Trust us to get the damn chapel".

Bryan asks, "Any volunteers to begin?".

A male tourist holds up his hand.

"Take a seat".

The tourist sits at the table.

Bryan begins, "If there is a presence, Spirit shall communicate through the radio device or make themselves known by manipulating the surroundings. The green dot device helps us see any movement".

The other tourists huddle together around the table.

"Flashlights off".

They turn off their flashlights.

"Feel free to ask questions".

The male tourist clears his throat, "Is anyone, erm, out there?".

The radio changes channels: Nothing but static...

Meanwhile, Shay and Deborah lead their group into the kitchen. A female tourist runs her finger along a large, oak table that rests in the middle. Shay asks, "Anyone done table tipping before?"
The female says, "Only with small tables, nothing this big".
"You'll know, of course, anyone can get a light table to move. It's the heavy ones that disprove trickery. Get ready to have your minds blown. Gather round".
The tourists gather around the oak table.
Deborah says, "Spread out evenly and place your fingertips lightly on the table edge".
The spirit tourists rest their fingers on the table. Shay and Deborah back away from the table.
"Tonight is yours to experience the paranormal and make up your own minds if this is real or not".
The spirit tourists seem nervous.
"Close your eyes. Picture a beacon of light at your very core. Force the light into your mind's eye. Propel the energy into the room around you. Feel the power surround you. Open yourselves up to Spirit. Spirit will open up to you..."
The table vibrates. The spirit tourists gasp in amazement.
"We are ready to begin..."

Elsewhere, Aaron and Leti lead their party into a Victorian school room with their flashlights. Wooden desks with joined chairs line the room in front of a teacher's table and black chalkboard.
Aaron jokes, "Ok, this is my worst nightmare. I hated school".
Leti plays, "Pupils, take a seat. Class will begin shortly".
"Yeah, I just got less fond of you".
The spirit tourists sit at the school tables. Aaron rubs the chalkboard clear with an eraser. Leti sits at the teacher's desk.
"Flashlights off".
The spirit tourists turn their flashlights off.
"We call out to spirit to make your presence known".
A female tourist asks, "Did you hear that?"

"Hear what?"
Nothing but silence…
The female continues, "It sounded like—"

An empty student tabletop suddenly flips up.

Spirit tourists turn their flashlights on in fear. Leti jumps as Aaron sits at a desk in front of her, "My God, don't do that".
"Do what?"
"I just didn't expect you to be sat right in front of me when the light came on, haha"
"My face ain't that scary is it?"

The spirit tourists discover that a tabletop is open…
"Ok, guys, keep your lights off this time. It heightens activity".
The spirit tourists turn their flashlights off…

 Back in the chapel, green dots scan the room as Bryan, Rob and the spirit tourists stand around the table. The seated male tourist asks, "Did this chapel belong to a priest?".
Bryan and Rob glance at each other in horror. *What are the odds he'd ask that? Of all things, he kicked off our séance with that???*

The radio crackles as it searches channels: no answer.
 "Does this thing even work?".

The radio scans channels and answers from several stations, flicking through channels at lightning speed to reveal an answer using different voices on radiowaves:

"Yes-- Without a doubt-- He is here-- Don't be afraid".

The tourists search for movement of green dot lights. Nothing yet.
"Ok. Thank you". The radio crackles through channels in answer:

"That's ok-- What's on the agenda-- tonight? "

The male tourist gulps, "Oh, man, this is creepy. Erm, sorry. Who am I talking to exactly?".

The radio offers only static.

"Are you a priest?"

"This-- is certainly-- no priest".

Bryan and Rob show visible relief.

"What would you call yourself?"

"A—sinner".

Something moves among the green dot lights in the room. Spirit tourists get scared.

  Meanwhile in the kitchen, Shay and Deborah observe the spirit tourists as the oak table tips onto two legs.
A tourist asks, "Who's doing that?"
Deborah boasts, "Look for yourself.
Tourists search underneath the table. Nothing. The oak table tips onto the other two legs unaided.
Shay calls, "Thank you, Spirit. But I'm sure you can do more than that. Spirit, make this table spin".
The oak table falls back onto all four legs. It grinds across the floor and tips onto one leg. Spirit tourists gasp in amazement. The oak table begins to spin slowly. Spirit tourists move around with the table. The oak table spins quicker. Spirit tourists struggle to keep up with the speed.
Shay demands, "Spirit, let us test your strength".
The oak table suddenly stops and stands on just one leg.
Shay tells the group, "Try pushing it down".
They all push the table down with both hands. The oak table strongly resists and impossibly does not move.

They all check underneath and still find nothing.

In the schoolroom, Leti sits at the teacher's desk in the dark as Aaron and the other spirit tourists sit at school desks. The open tabletop slams down. Spirit tourists squeal.
Leti says, "Keep the lights off guys".
A female tourist asks, "Who's doing that?"
Leti explains, "He's here".
Footsteps move around the classroom.
"Oh no, oh no, oh no…"
"Stay calm everyone".

A tourist disobeys and scans the room with her flashlight in fear: Everyone is still sat at their own desk.
Leti requests, "Turn it off please".
"Thought it was one of you up to some trick".
The tourist turns their flashlight off.

A foot taps on the floor next to the tourist as if they are in trouble with a teacher. All of the tabletops spring open. The spirit tourists scream in the darkness. Footsteps walk towards the teacher's desk. Chalk screeches across the chalkboard.

Then silence…
Leti advises, "Ok, lights on".
Spirit tourists turn on their flashlights. They discover the open tabletops and a message on the board reads: 'GET OUT'.
All of the tabletops suddenly slam shut.
Aaron, Leti and the spirit tourists run out of the classroom.

Elsewhere, Bryan and Rob lead their tourists into the billiards room with their flashlights.
Rob asks, "Anyone fancy a game?"
A ball pockets itself unassisted. The group stops in their step.
Bryan laughs, "This is crazy. So much activity already".
Rob says, "I have an idea", and leaves the room.

The spirit tourists sniff the air. One of them announces, "My Grandad used to smoke cigars back in the day".

Rob enters and carries a pen, a large piece of paper and a wheeled, wooden instrument. He moves the balls and lays the items on the table. Rob asks, "Ever heard of a Spirit scribe?"

The spirit tourists gather around the table. Rob puts the pen in a holder and the wheels on the paper.

"Works like a Ouija board except Spirit can write or draw with our help. Fingers on the board".

The spirit tourists rest their fingers on the board.

Bryan requests, "Lights out. Stops the cheats from deliberately writing. If we can't see it, we know we didn't write it... Right?".

The spirit tourists turn their flashlights off.

Bryan asks, "Will any Spirit communicate with us? Use the instrument as you wish".

The wheels move. The instrument rolls. The pen draws something onto the paper. The wheels stop.

Bryan turns his flashlight on and reveals the drawing: A penis cartoon is drawn in pen. The spirit tourists howl with laughter.

"Ok, looks like we have a mischievous spirit on our hands..."

Meanwhile, Aaron and Leti lead their tourists into an ornate library. Books line the walls in floor-to-ceiling bookshelves. A work desk and leather chair sit at one end.

Leti explains, "Let's keep the lights on this time".

Aaron chimes in, "Good idea".

The spirit tourists search the library with newfound courage.

One of the tourists demands, "Make something happen. That was exhilarating. Do something more impressive!"

Leti seems concerned, "Let's tone things down a bit".

The tourist demands, "That's not what we're paying for", as they start running their fingers along dusty books. Leti stands by Aaron, clearly afraid and losing control over her own group.

The tourist demands, "Spirit, wake up. We wanna play".

Leti begs, "Please don't".

Aaron requests, "Leave the questioning to us this time please".

The tourist ignores Aaron and Leti. She begins to move books around, "Ooooh, is that gonna piss Spirit off?"

Silence.

They demand, "If you don't do something soon, I'm gonna damage all your books. They'd make a nice fire...", as they flick on their lighter near the bookcase as a threat. Leti hurries out of the library.

Aaron suggests, "Sorry guys, just take a breather for a minute. I'll check on her".

In the dark corridor, Leti cries to herself. Aaron finds Leti and holds her close.

"Can't even control my own group".

"Don't worry, babe".

"I'm scared. Something's off. This place is horrible".

"We'll regroup with the others soon. Things are gettin' out of hand".

The other spirit tourists wait, unattended, in the library. The demanding tourist knocks a book to the floor.

The leather chair slides back as if something unseen stands up from it.

All of the books in the bookcase fly from their shelves, untouched, and hit the spirit tourists. The spirit tourists scream and flee the room. The door locks them inside so they cannot escape.

Aaron and Leti hear the door bang repeatedly. They try to open it but the door is locked from the other side. Shay and Deborah, Bryan and Rob, along with their groups, sprint to meet Aaron and Leti in the corridor.

Shay asks, "What's going on?"

Deborah explains, "We heard screaming".

Aaron informs, "They're locked inside".

Rob hurries with the keys and unlocks the door. The spirit tourists pour into the corridor. The demanding tourist accuses, "You left us. It attacked us. This was your fault".

Leti sticks up for herself, "I told you to stop".
"You're paid to protect us".
"You provoked Spirit".
"We could press charges".
"Good luck with that.
"I demand my money back".
Shay looks concerned. Deborah intervenes, "Call me a psychic but that's not in your future either".
"They're not in control here, guys. I'm off. If you've got half a brain cell you'd leave with me too".
Shay tries to regain control, "Look, we'll regroup. I'll lead".
"Who's leaving with me?".
The majority of the spirit tourists nod their heads.
Shay complains, "We ain't even tried the tombs yet".
"You're gettin' bad feedback on Facebook for this".
The majority of the group leaves the building. Deborah addresses the tourists that stay, "Let's take a break".
Shay adds, "Means more food for the rest of us". 72.

The few remaining Spirit Tourists pick at a banquet of snacks. Shay gathers Aaron, Leti, Deborah, Bryan and Rob in a corner.
Shay asks, "What happened back there?"
Leti admits, "I left the room".
"Never leave them unattended."
"They wouldn't listen. We'd seen a fair amount of shit go down in the schoolroom. Thought it would calm 'em down but it did the opposite. That bitch started threatening to damage books. She angered Spirit".
Bryan agrees, "I've noticed things are kicking off all around the building. We should really bring things to a close".
Shay orders, "Hell no. This is our last night. The cellars are waiting. Those tombs will save the night.

After their snack banquet is over, Shay leads Deborah, Bryan, Aaron, Leti, Rob and the remaining spirit tourists down the dark, stone, cellar staircase. The tourists panic as they descend into darkness.
"Any lights down here?"

"Darkness adds to the atmosphere".
"I can't see a thing".
"It heightens the senses. Rob can be our eyes".

 Rob gets out his night vision camera and films.
Someone says, "I've got a bad fee—" and then screams. Rob points
the camera at the tourist in question. They writhe and twist in pain.
"Something scratched me. Oh my God. Get me outta here!"
Shay requests, "Wait!".

 The spirit tourists flee up the stairs and emerge from the staircase.
Shay chases them. One of the tourists lifts her shirt and reveals deep,
bloody, fingernail scratches on her side and back, "We're done. This is
fucked up". The spirit tourists leave the building.

 Rob comes out of nowhere and makes Shay jump. He locks the front
door and pockets the keys, "Good riddance. They don't have to spoil
our evening. We can get footage for the channel. Have a solo scout
for a change. Just us professionals..."
Shay and Rob descend the staircase. Rob turns to fix a motion
detector trip wire across the doorway at the top of the stairs.
"Since we're on our own now. Can't be too careful..."
"Good idea".

 Shay and Rob join Deborah, Bryan, Leti and Aaron on the cellar
staircase. Bryan asks, "We callin' it quits?".
Rob checks his watch, "We've got a few more hours left".
Shay suggests, "There's no way I'm giving up after all that. Would be a
wasted trip. AND it's our last night in this country..."
Deborah supports, "Will be good for the website".
Shay adds, "Takes me back to our early days when it was just us".
Leti requests, "Can we wait outside?"
Shay rejects, "Come off it. We stick together".
Rob explains, "Was down here on my own before we started. You'll
love what I found".
The group descends the cellar staircase.

Rob films the bloody finger marks on the wall, "Reckon one of the other tourists scratched her?".
Bryan shakes his head, Unfortunately not. Something else is lurking down here".
Leti clings to Aaron. Rob peeks the night vision camera into the cellar. The night vision reveals a network of low-ceiling tunnels that branch off into various chambers. Deborah and Shay peek at Rob's viewfinder, intrigued.
Shay asks, "Think this was where they kept those injured soldiers?"
Deborah states, "With all that room upstairs? I doubt it".
"Maybe just the dead ones then".
Rob edges into the tunnel network. The others follow him.
Bryan suggests, "Most likely used for storage".
"Of bodies?"
"Food supplies probably".

The night vision camera reveals various empty storage rooms.
Shay orders, "Capture everything".
Rob reassures, "Don't worry, I will".
"I read these tunnels are older than the Institute itself. These weren't accessed by the Victorians. They were sealed off".
"Why?"
"No idea".

Rob reveals a bricked up chamber door, "Only one way to find out".
Rob pulls a chisel from his pocket.
Bryan seems surprised, "You carry a chisel around with you?"
Rob coldly explains, "For protection".
Rob rests the chisel against the brick. Shay grabs Rob's arm. Rob warns Shay with a glare.
Shay demands, "Any damage is coming outta your paycheck".
Rob states, "Fine by me".
Bryan warns, "I'm not sure about this. What do you think's in there?"
Shay explains, "These foundations date back to the 17th century. Could be anything".
Aaron asks, "Servant quarters?"

Leti asks, "Why would they brick it up though?"
Aaron says, "I don't wanna know".

 Rob thrusts the camera at Bryan. Rob chisels at the bricked up door.
Aaron laughs, "Now who's the Victorian sicko?"
Rob asks, "Do you want footage or not?"
Aaron asks, "17th century. That's 1600s right?"
Shay says, "Tunnels date back to 1666".
Leti, "Oh that's just typical…"

 Rob breaks a hole into the brick wall. Bryan peeks the night vision
camera through: Brick dust blocks all sight of the room's contents.
Rob chips a narrow gap in the brickwork door and peers in.
Rob asks, "Leti?"
"No way am I goin' in there".
"Take one for the team".
"I'm not taking anything. You're not even a part of the team".
Aaron suggests, "If it's been over 350 years, there's nothing in there
that'll get ya, Leti. Unless you believe in zombies…".
"Oh, sure, 'cos that's stopped everything else happening tonight".
Rob demands, "You're the only one who'll fit".
Leti squeezes past Rob and snatches the camera, "Anything happens
to me it's on your head".
She slips through the gap. The dust settles in the room and Leti
chokes from the smell. She discovers rotten toys for a girl.
Leti states, "What the-- Why would they brick up a child's room?"
She blows dust from one of the toys and discovers a name carved into
it. Leti pulls a lighter from her pocket to read: 'Elsa Lloyd'.
"Noooooooo waaaaaaaay".

The flame reveals the preserved corpse of a little girl in the corner
with her mouth sewn shut.

Leti screams and clambers out of the room. She reaches the group on
the other side of the brick door. "There's a body in there! Still
preserved. I think the fact it was bricked up kept the climate right".

Bryan picks up the chiselled brick from the floor. He takes the camera off Leti, spits on the brick and views the remains of red paint.

Bryan sighs, "Oh no. How terrible".

Leti asks, "What?"

Bryan explains, "Plague victim. They used to mark the doors of the afflicted. 1666 was when the Black Death ravaged this country. I read that families would brick up their ill relatives to stop it spreading from town to town. Must've been servants".

Leti asks, "Then why's her mouth sewn shut?".

A banshee screams from further down the tunnel.

Shay snatches the camera from Bryan, thrusts it at Rob and leads the group further into the tunnel with a flashlight.. He kicks up dust with his boot, films with a night vision camera and jokes around, "Look... Orbs..."

Leti coughs, pulls an inhaler from her bag and uses it. Aaron puts his arm around Leti and barges Rob ahead. Bryan warns the group, "Enough. I sense a growing malice in the vicinity".

Shay guides the group into a cellar chamber with fearless, childish excitement, "Perfect. Get in. Quietly".

Deborah, Bryan, Leti, Aaron and Rob funnel into the tiny area...

Aaron complains, "It's a bit of a tight fit".

Rob jokes, "That's what she said!".

Deborah grabs Rob's arm as he holds the camera, "Stop pissing about. Get footage for the channel. The less talking from you, the better".

They kneel and sit in the sandy cellar chamber.

Shay begins his séance, "Spirit, we are humbled by your presence. I wish to push further as I feel your strength growing..."

Shay picks up a pebble from the ground, "I'll throw this pebble outside the chamber. I want you to throw it back. Got me in focus, Rob?".

Rob jests, "Yeah, you look like Brad Pitt... If he put on sixty pounds".

Shay raises his eyebrow, "...Spirit, I'm throwing the pebble now".

Shay throws the pebble out of the chamber into the tunnel. They hear the pebble hit a wall. The group grows anxious.

Something throws the pebble back into the room! It rolls through the sand in front of Shay. Leti squeals. Shay laughs.

Leti whispers, "Oh my God. Oh my God, it's happening..."
Shay asks, "Did you get that in frame?".
Rob answers, "Fuck me. Er... Yeah... Got it... This is goin' viral".

The group moves further into the chamber, away from the door, unsurprisingly unnerved by whatever has followed them down to the tunnels... Or whatever was present before they got down here...

Bryan warns, "Shay—"
Shay ignores, "Thank you, Spirit. Let's get even more activity" and reaches for the pebble to throw it again, sensing how many more subscribers tonight's episode will be netted by this sensationalism.
Bryan advises, "Let's call it a night".
Shay barks, "Hell no. This is EXACTLY why we're here".
Leti complains, "It's freakin' me out, guys".

Rob searches outside with the night vision viewfinder: Nothing is seen but dust in the air of the tunnel.
Shay implores, "Emerge, Spirit. We feel your force. Come!".
Shay throws the pebble out of the room again. The pebble flies back inside and hits Shay's jacket harder.
Deborah gasps, "Amazing".
Leti begs, "Please stop".
Shay boasts, "Oh, we ain't seen nothing yet—"

Scratches at a large stone block on the floor are heard.

Shay scoffs at the Spirit to try and get better reactions for his vlog, "Spirit... This is pathetic. You're weak. Pebble barely touched me. Show us your true strength. Or are we stronger than you because we are still alive?"

...Silence.

Leti panics, "Spirit's gone. Let's get ou—"

The block flies through the air and caves in Shay's skull! The crew members flee for their lives and escape the room as fast as they can. Rob drops the camera.

It films as blood leaks from Shay's head into the sand.

Deborah leads the escape through the pitch black tunnels. Aaron, Leti, Bryan and Rob follow but can't see. Deborah scrambles ahead and wails in sorrow, mourning her dead husband. The roof of the cellar corridor groans.
Leti calls, "Deborah, slow down".
The roof begins to crumble.
"Deb! Watch out!".
A section of the roof collapses and crushes Deborah to death.

Leti screams as Aaron drags her over Deborah's corpse. Bryan clambers over the rocks. Rob is lost in the commotion. Bryan pushes past Aaron and Leti and hurries up the stairs. Aaron and Leti follow. Still no sign of Rob... Bryan rushes out of the cellar staircase. He trips on the motion detector wire, pummels into a stone column and breaks his neck. Blood leaks from his head.

Leti and Aaron appear from the stairs. They reach the main door but it's locked. Aaron suggests, "There's a back door". Aaron and Leti sprint through the foyer into the corridor. Aaron falls behind Leti. "Rob? Rob!?".
No answer.
Leti sprints too fast towards a different staircase. Aaron runs backwards and searches for Rob: no sign. "Rob?! Where are ya?". Leti reaches the stairwell and halts in fear. She spots the priest dressed in white at the bottom of the stairs and screams. Aaron crashes into Leti and they tumble down the staircase...

Rob runs out of the cellar stairs and slips on Bryan's blood. He sprints to the main door: it's locked. He pulls the key from his pocket, unlocks the door and sprints out of the building. Outside, Rob hurries into the empty darkness of the Victorian estate. He pauses and turns to view the open, oak door.

"Leti? Aaron?"

Silence.

Rob tiptoes towards the door. He peers inside at the darkness of the foyer.

"Aaron? Leti!? Fuck".

Rob pushes the oak door open slowly. Moonlight reveals Bryan's corpse. He spots bloody footprints that lead in the other direction.

"Shit, shit. Time to man up, Rob".

Rob slaps himself in the face for adrenaline.

"This is a bad idea, man. Fuck. Aaron, don't make me do this, dude!"

Rob edges into the foyer. He picks up a heavy, metal candlestick from the side and raises it above his head. Rob kneels to pick up Bryan's flashlight. He shines the light and inches into the dark corridor.

"Shitting myself, guys, answer me!"

Rob reaches the end of the corridor and turns the corner. The front door slowly creaks shut with the wind. Rob shuffles along the corridor to the edge of the staircase.

"Guys?"

Rob scans the staircase with the flashlight. Light reveals a white sheet that covers the figure of a man at the bottom of the stairs. Rob descends as he focuses the flashlight on the sheet. He reaches the figure, pulls the sheet and reveals a statue. It was never the Priest, only a trick of the light... As the sheet falls to the floor, Rob spots the dead bodies of Aaron and Leti, in a final embrace, at the bottom of the stairs. Rob observes the dead couple unflinchingly.

"So young... Oh, well..."

He pulls something from his backpack: Rob takes a Polaroid photo of the two corpses and relaxes. Rob leans over to a light switch and turns it on. A chandelier pours light into the stairwell.

Rob pauses to dig at blood and skin under his fingernails. He had clearly been the one to scratch the female spirit tourist in the dark earlier...

Rob confidently strides through the building, as if there was never anything to be afraid of in the first place. Almost as if he feels at home. He detaches the trip wire from the floor and pockets it. Rob photographs Bryan's corpse with the Polaroid camera. Rob flicks the cellar stair lights on and descends.

Rob holds a flashlight in his mouth and fans the polaroid photos so they develop. He trudges through the tunnel. Rob reaches the bottom and pulls a rope on the ceiling. The collapsed ceiling section appears to be a trap door that he had arranged. Rob puts on gloves to remove rocks from Deborah's corpse. He throws the rocks into the side rooms. Rob photographs Deborah's body.

Rob reaches the chamber and views Shay's body with disdain. "Should've listened to my ideas, you prick. That band didn't and look what I had to do to them... Could've taken us places. Now fuckin' look at ya. Look what I had to do... It's all your fault. Scumbag".

Rob buries his heel into Shay's skull and spits on him. He photographs his boot in Shay's head. Rob puts the Polaroid camera in his backpack. He shines a flashlight at the stone block catapult in the corner of the room. Rob whistles an upbeat tune as he packs the catapult away. The flashlight flickers. He hits it in frustration.

He drops the flashlight and picks up the bloody night vision camera from the sand. He scans the cellar chamber with the camera: nothing. "Mind's playin' tricks on ya, Rob".

Rob takes the memory card out of the camera and pockets it. He picks up a hidden tape recorder, rewinds it, plays the banshee screams and chuckles to himself.

But Rob hears scratching at the stone block...

"Oh, fuck off".

 He sticks the recorder into his backpack and scans the room with the camera once again. The viewfinder reveals orbs as they float around the room. "God damn orbs".

The generator cuts out... Water pipes gurgle to a halt... The cellar stair lights go out...

 Rob gets anxious, switches the camera to night vision and scans the dark emptiness around him.

Silence except Rob's heavy breathing.

Until, something scratches Rob's eye and cheek. He covers his face in agony and drops the camera.

The camera films a pebble as it rolls into the chamber from the tunnel. It leaves a trail of blood in the sand.

 Rob lets out a guttural scream. Sounds of commotion echo through the chamber. Something crashes to the floor with a heavy thud.

Silence and total darkness.

The unseen ghost of Elsa Lloyd giggles and then bursts into song, as her voice echoes through the estate:

"Ring-a-ring o' roses,
A pocket full of posies,
A-tishoo! A-tishoo!
We all fall down..."

the end

Other Written Works by Tadhg Culley

Novellas – Available on Amazon
'The Poet And The Prostitute'
'The Holler Screams'
'Gridlock Deadlock'
'Urban Expiration'
'Coming Soon To Cinemas Near You'
'Mirror's Eye Motel'

Short Story Collection – Available on Amazon
'Secrets Buried In The Woods'

Memoir – Available on Amazon
'Paperback Silverback'

Poetry Books – Available on Amazon
'The Complete Poetical Works Of Tadhg Culley' (Collection of 288 poems)
'Undo the Heartbreak' (Anthology of 150 poems)
'Unsung Lyricality' (Anthology of 68 poems)
'Relive the Romance' (Chapbook of 34 poems)
'Red Glows Only Lovers Know' (1 long poem)
'Melancholic Moments' (Chapbook of 21 poems)
'Shards Of A Ceramic Soul' (Chapbook of 15 poems)
'True Love Might (Not) Exist' (Chapbook of 7 poems)

Feature Film Screenplays
'Endless Life' (Realist Drama)
'Cold Star' (Gritty Drama)
'Stepping Stones' (Thriller/Horror)
'Tailback' (Thriller)
'Urbex' (Thriller)
'Quarrying Souls' (Supernatural Horror)
'The Long Barrow' (Archaeological Horror)
'Mouth of the Hollow' (Revenge Thriller)
'In Cinemas Now' (Supernatural Horror)

About the Author

Tadhg Culley is a Professional Screenwriter, Published Author and Poet from the UK. He has written ten feature film screenplays, eight TV series scripts, eight poetry books, seven novellas, three guidebooks, one memoir, one collection of short stories, and many other short-form works, delving into documentary, theatre, animation and games. He is a BAFTA Scholar and graduate of both the National Film & TV School (NFTS) & the University of Creative Arts (UCA).

Printed in Great Britain
by Amazon

66362204R00041